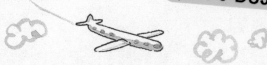

Some say the Loch Ness Monster is a prehistoric sea creature. Other people think it's a silly old superstition.

Locals call the creature Nessie. They search for her by plane, in boats, and even on a Nessie Cam.

Thousands of people claim to have seen the Loch Ness Monster. Scientists are skeptical. What do you think?

43 Old Cemetery Road: Book Seven

# The Loch Ness Punster

Kate Klise
Illustrated by M. Sarah Klise

Houghton Mifflin Harcourt
Boston New York

www.hmhco.com

The Library of Congress has cataloged the hardcover edition as follows:
Klise, Kate.
Loch Ness punster / by Kate Klise ; illustrated by M. Sarah Klise.
pages cm.— (43 Old Cemetery Road ; book 7)
Summary: Twelve-year-old Seymour Hope and his ghostly "mother," Olive, go to Scotland to claim a
castle inherited from Ignatius Grumply's punster uncle, Ian, but while they tend an aged tortoise and
face an unscrupulous developer, Iggie deals with Ian's ghost and an inept insurance agent.
[1. Letters—Fiction. 2. Ghosts—Fiction. 3. Uncles—Fiction. 4. Inheritance and succession—Fiction. 5.
Turtles—Fiction. 6. Scotland—Fiction. 7. Humorous stories.] I. Klise, M. Sarah, illustrator. II. Title.
PZ7.K684Loc 2015
[Fic]—dc23
2014015884
Designed by M. Sarah Klise

ISBN: 978-0-544-31337-8 hardcover
ISBN: 978-0-544-81085-3 paperback

Manufactured in the United States
DOC 10 9 8 7 6 5 4 3 2 1
4500613454

Those who don't believe in magic will never find it.
Roald Dahl

# Welcome to Spence Mansion

If you've visited before, you know Spence Mansion is a
32½-room house in Ghastly, Illinois.
It was built by Olive C. Spence in 1874.
She lived here until her death in 1911.

She's still here.

Can you see
her opera glasses
in the cupola?

Olive C. Spence is a ghost.

But you already knew that.

You also probably know that Seymour Hope was abandoned by his parents when he was eleven years old.

Lucky for Seymour, he was adopted by Olive C. Spence and Ignatius B. Grumply, a man who is often as grumpy as his name suggests.

Together, this trio is creating the world's most popular ghost story, *43 Old Cemetery Road*. The book is published three chapters at a time and sent to readers by mail.

43 Old Cemetery Road

Olive C. Spence, Ignatius B. Grumply and Seymour Hope

Olive and Ignatius write the words. Seymour draws the pictures.

Where do they find inspiration? Everywhere!

So far they've published chapters about Seymour's parents, Olive's best friend, Ignatius's former fiancée, and other assorted villains and scoundrels.

But there's one subject they've never explored in their book. It's a topic they've never even discussed as a family.

It was something Seymour had been wondering about for more than a year, ever since he first met Ignatius B. Grumply.

He finally asked it in a letter one summer day.

Dear Iggy,

Why are you always so grumpy?

—Seymour

To answer that question, you must know about Iggy's childhood.
And you *will* when you read a letter that arrived from Scotland not long ago.

→

**DR. IAN GRUMPLY**
**Psychiatrist**
Specializing in Humor Research & Laugh Therapy

43 Old Castle Road
Loch Ness, Scotland

July 2

Ignatius B. Grumply
43 Old Cemetery Road
Ghastly, Illinois USA

Dear Ignatius,

I just finished reading *43 Old Cemetery Road*. What a delight!
I had no idea you'd adopted a boy named Seymour, or that
you were writing a book with the ghost of Olive C. Spence.
How exciting!

I've been doing some writing, too. I just completed the final
draft of my last will and testament. You know what a will is,
don't you? A dead giveaway. Ha ha!

But seriously, as you know, I've never married or had children.
My only brother is deceased. I have no living cousins. No aunts,
uncles, nieces, or nephews—except you, Ignatius. When I
die, you will inherit everything I own, including my home in
Loch Ness. I bought a castle here years ago with you in mind.
I thought Loch Ness would be a perfect place for us to talk
about myths and monsters.

It's unfortunate that we haven't spoken in many years, but I
hope you'll come visit so we can patch things up. Bring the
whole family! I'd love to meet Olive and Seymour.

I suggest you hurry, as I don't have many days left. I'm almost out of jokes, too. Here's one you might like: What do you call an old psychiatrist who's on his last breath? A *sigh*-chiatrist. Ha!

Yours with a smile,

Uncle Ian

Uncle Ian

P.S. If I don't hear from you before I die, your next of kin will inherit everything I own, including Grumply Castle.

# IGNATIUS B. GRUMPLY

#### A WRITER IN RESIDENCE

July 9

Dr. Ian Grumply
43 Old Castle Road
Loch Ness, Scotland


Dear Uncle Ian,

I have no desire to see your castle or hear any more of your terrible jokes. Please do not contact me again.

Why must you always be such a grouch?

Olive, please. I'm trying to write a personal letter. Can I have a little privacy?

If you'll tell me why you're being so rude to an elderly relative.

You don't know my uncle.

No, I don't. Stop scowling and tell me. Who is Dr. Ian Grumply?

He's a world-famous psychiatrist. I spent every summer with him from the age of twelve until I left for college.

Fascinating! You've never told me anything about your childhood.

I don't like talking about it or Uncle Ian. He was the world's *worst* uncle.

But consider this: Your uncle is Seymour's great-uncle. It might be nice for our son to meet a relative. And Scotland is beautiful. I haven't been there since I was twelve. My family took a summer vacation to the Scottish Highlands in 1830. Iggy, *we* should take a family vacation.

I hate family vacations.

You'd rather stay home and keep doing the same thing month after month, year after year, and never take any time off for fun?

Yes.

Good grief. Don't you know life is for *living?*

Now you sound like Uncle Ian. That was one of his favorite sayings.

The more I hear about your uncle, the more I like the man.

You can like him all you want. I don't have to.

But aren't you *curious* about Grumply Castle? Don't you want to see Loch Ness?

I have no interest in Loch Ness or anything tha

Iggy, someone's knocking at the front door.

Who is it?

I don't know, but I see a truck parked at the curb. It says *International Telegram Service.*

Who would send a telegram in this day and age?

I have no idea. Go to the door and find out!

# INTERNATIONAL
# TELEGRAM SERVICE

**To:** IGNATIUS B. GRUMPLY
**Fr:** LOCH NESS LAW FIRM

JULY 9

IAN GRUMPLY DIED PEACEFULLY
IN HIS SLEEP TODAY = STOP =
PLEASE SEND SEYMOUR HOPE TO
SCOTLAND IMMEDIATELY TO CLAIM
HIS INHERITANCE = STOP

# ➤THE GHASTLY TIMES◄

Friday, July 10
Cliff Hanger, Editor

*"We're Living in Ghastly Times"*

50 cents
Afternoon Edition

## Hope Inherits Castle in Scotland

Seymour Hope never met his great-uncle Ian Grumply. But the 12-year-old Ghastly boy is the sole heir to everything the late Dr. Ian Grumply owned, including a castle in Loch Ness, Scotland.

"I'm so excited to see it!" said a delighted Hope. "I've never been to Scotland or seen a real live castle. I just wish Iggy were coming with us."

"No thanks," said Ignatius B. Grumply, who will remain at Spence Mansion, working on new chapters of the family's bestselling book, *43 Old Cemetery Road*. "Olive suggested I write about my past," said Grumply. "She thinks I should call the new installment 'Growing Up Grumply.'"

What about the family's majority rule policy, which states that whenever all three residents of Spence Mansion can't agree on a particular course of action, they do whatever two residents want to do?

"That," snapped Grumply, "applies to business decisions only. Grumply Castle

**Hope and Spence will travel to Scotland without Grumply.**

is Seymour's personal business. If it were up to me, I'd sell the castle and be done with it. Who in the world wants to live in Scotland?"

Scotland is part of the United Kingdom. It occupies the northern third of the island of Great Britain and is governed by a constitutional monarchy. Queen Elizabeth is Scotland's current head of state.

## Library Launches Borrow-a-Pet Program

**Balm borrows pets from Lyve.**

Want to borrow a puppy for the summer? How about a kitten, gerbil, hamster, bird or snake?

Starting today, the Ghastly Public Library will lend those pets and others to anyone with a library card.

"I'm always looking for new summer programs to offer our patrons," said M. Balm, chief librarian. "This year I thought it would be fun to let people borrow pets, so I contacted Barry A. Lyve at the Ghastly Pet Store."

*Continued on page 2, column 1*

**LIBRARY** *Continued from page 1, column 2*

Lyve, a lifelong library supporter, was all for it. "It's a great way to try out a new pet," he said. "Plus, this means I can close the shop and go on vacation. It'll be the first time in 35 years."

Lyve left last night on a trip to Hawaii after moving his collection of animals to the Ghastly Public Library.

One Ghastly resident has already been to the library to borrow a pet. "Seymour Hope arrived first thing this morning to get Mr. Poe," said Balm.

Mr. Poe is a 198-year-old giant tortoise that has lived at the Ghastly Pet Store for decades.

# New Insurance Company Opens in Ghastly

**Garren Teed will insure anything.**

Ask Garren Teed who needs insurance, and his answer is emphatic: *Everyone.*

"Insurance is the best way to protect yourself and your family from life's unfortunate events," explained Teed, an authorized insurance agent for We Insure Anything, Inc. "Here's how it works," he said. "You agree to pay me a reasonable fee every month. Then, if something terrible happens—say, your house burns down or you get into a car accident—I give you money to repair or replace your home or car. It's that simple!"

Teed is offering home, health, auto and life insurance policies. He was recently transferred from the We Insure Anything home office in Davenport, Iowa, after failing to meet his sales quota.

# SEYMOUR HOPE
## Illustrator in Residence

43 Old Cemetery Road
Third Floor
Ghastly, Illinois

July 11

M. Balm
Ghastly Public Library
12 Scary Street
Ghastly, Illinois

Dear Mr. Balm,

Thanks for letting me borrow Mr. Poe. I'll take good care of him. I'm really looking forw

Darling, we leave for Scotland tomorrow.

Hi, Olive! I didn't know you were still awake. Can't Mr. Poe come with us?

He's awfully old, dear. Traveling can be difficult for the elderly.

Is that why Iggy doesn't want to go to Scotland with us?

I'm not sure. Iggy has been unusually grumpy lately. That letter from his uncle upset him terribly. Perhaps we'll learn why when we get to Scotland.

I can't believe Iggy doesn't want to go on vacation.

Nor can I. But your father is a neophobe.

What's that?

A neophobe is a person who fears new things. I, on the other hand, am a neophiliac. Can you guess what that means? Keep in mind *neo* means "new" in Greek and *philos* means "love."

Is a neophiliac someone who loves new things?

Exactly. Unlike your father, I enjoy trying new things, going new places, having new experiences. It makes me feel less dead.

Am I a neophobe or a neophiliac?

I'm not sure, dear. Time will tell.

What do you want me to be, Olive?

I want you to be someone who embraces change and has an appetite for adventure. Iggy never seemed to acquire the knack for trying new things. He reminds me of that tortoise who hides in his shell and rarely budges. But there's a whole *world* out there to explore. My job as your mother is to help you grow into the most interesting, curious young man you can be. Isn't that what you want, too?

I guess so.

Good! Because fortune favors the bold.

What does that mean?

It means good things come to those who take chances—and to those of us who take vacations. So pack your things. You may use my old trunk as your suitcase.

What should I pack?

Your passport, good walking shoes, and comfortable clothes. Please pack some art supplies, too. I'd like you to chronicle our vacation in illustrated letters to Iggy so he can see what a glorious time we're having. But first, please call Mr. Balm at home. Tell him that Iggy will care for Mr. Poe while we're gone. I'll make our travel arrangements.

Olive, are you going to buy a plane ticket? You could probably sneak on without being noticed, like you did when we went to Hollywood.

I know, darling, but I want to make sure I get a seat this time. It's a long flight. I only wish I hadn't let my passport expire. No matter. I'm sure I have something I can use for identification. I'll search while you pack.

# STATE OF ILLINOIS
## CERTIFICATE OF DEATH

NAME OF DECEASED

(First)     (Middle)     (Last)

Olive     Christine     Spence

RESIDENCE OF DECEASED

(Street address)     (City)     (State)

43 Old Cemetery Road     Ghastly     IL

DATE OF DEATH

(Month)     (Date)     (Year)

May     5     1911

*Notary Public*
**State of Illinois**
May 5, 1911

AGE AT THE TIME OF DEATH

93

OCCUPATION OF THE DECEASED

Writer

CAUSE OF DEATH

A broken heart caused by the continued rejection of New York publishers

This is a true and actual certificate of death that must be honored by all men and women.

GHASTLY
*SPEARMINT*
GUM

# HEIR AIRLINES

## Hope/Seymour

BOARDING PASS
July 12

440
FROM Ghastly, IL (GAS)
TO Loch Ness, Scotland (NSY)

GATE 7
BOARDS AT 7:50 AM
SEAT 32A

# HEIR AIRLINES

## Spence/Olive C.

BOARDING PASS
July 12

SEATING
2

440
FROM Ghastly, IL (GAS)
TO Loch Ness, Scotland (NSY)

GATE 7
DEPARTS AT 8:20 AM

SEAT 32A

Y-CABIN
037 2458373621

TKT

CONFIRMATION NBR J6660C
037 2458373621 CPN 1
ISSUED BY U201999 AT FFDF47 PHXGS

PRINTED IN U.S.A. BY MAGNETIC TICKET AND LABEL CORP., DALLAS, TX    PO857    RUN 10-11

RUN 10-11

STAPLE HERE

Do not expose to excessive heat or direct sunlight.

Hope/Seymour

440
FROM Ghastly, IL (GAS)
TO Loch Ness, Scotland (NSY)

GATE 7
DEPARTS AT 8:20 AM

Spence/Olive C.

440
FROM Ghastly, IL (GAS)
TO Loch Ness, Scotland (NSY)

GATE 7
DEPARTS AT 8:20 AM

SEAT 32A

CPN-1

July 12

Dear Iggy,

I'm writing this on the plane to Scotland. Olive and I are sitting next to each other. The flight attendant brought me dinner a little while ago (pasta with chicken), but he didn't bring anything for Olive. I asked for a second meal so she could have something to eat.

I wish you were coming with us. But since you're not, I decided to bring the next best thing: Mr. Poe. Olive says he reminds her of you. He fit perfectly in Olive's old trunk. Luckily, there are some holes in it, so he'll be able to breathe. I hope Mr. Poe doesn't mind traveling in the luggage compartment.

The plane is scheduled to land in less than three hours. I'll write more when we get to Scotland.

Love,

—Seymour

P.S. Please don't tell Olive I brought Mr. Poe. She thinks I left him with you.

# GHASTLY PUBLIC LIBRARY

12 SCARY STREET.........................GHASTLY, ILLINOIS
M. BALM................................................CHIEF LIBRARIAN

July 15

Ignatius B. Grumply
43 Old Cemetery Road
Ghastly, Illinois

Dear Ignatius,

Are you sitting down? If not, please do.

Barry A. Lyve just called from Hawaii. He said he was having second thoughts about the Borrow-a-Pet Program. I assured him that our patrons are very responsible. "I can't imagine anyone losing or damaging your pets," I said. "But if someone does, the library will reimburse you for your losses."

That's when Barry said, "Okay, just don't lend Mr. Poe to anyone. That tortoise is worth ten thousand dollars."

*Ten thousand dollars?* I nearly fainted. I'm still trembling as I write these words, but I wanted to let you know so you can return Mr. Poe to the library immediately. I'll keep him safe until Barry returns from Hawaii.

Sincerely stressed out,

*M. Balm*

M. Balm

# IGNATIUS B. GRUMPLY

A WRITER IN RESIDENCE

43 OLD CEMETERY ROAD        2ND FLOOR        GHASTLY, ILLINOIS

July 16

Mr. M. Balm
Ghastly Public Library
12 Scary Street
Ghastly, Illinois


Dear M. Balm,

I can't return Mr. Poe to the library. Seymour took the blasted tortoise to Scotland.

Don't worry. I'll assume full responsibility. If anything happens to the tortoise, I'll pay the Ghastly Pet Store ten thousand dollars. Let's just hope *nothing* happens.

Sincerely responsible,

*Ignatius B. Grumply*

Ignatius B. Grumply

P.S. I wonder if I could buy a pet insurance policy.

# IGNATIUS B. GRUMPLY

### A WRITER IN RESIDENCE

43 OLD CEMETERY ROAD        2ND FLOOR        GHASTLY, ILLINOIS

July 17

Mr. Garren Teed
We Insure Anything, Inc.
10 Scary Street
Ghastly, Illinois


Dear Mr. Teed,

Do you offer pet insurance? If so, I'd like to buy a
ten-thousand-dollar policy for an elderly tortoise
named Mr. Poe.

Please send the paperwork to 43 Old Cemetery
Road for my signature.

Sincerely,

*Ignatius B. Grumply*

Ignatius B. Grumply

# GARREN TEED
## We Insure Anything, Inc.

July 20

Mr. Ichabod B. Grumpy
43 Old Cemetery Road
Ghastly, Illinois

Dear Mr. Grumpy,

Congratulations! You're my first customer. Or you *will* be my first customer, as soon as you buy a policy.

I need to call the home office in Iowa to find out if we offer tortoise insurance. But here's something I *know* I can sell you today: life insurance. If you're worried about an elderly tortoise, you're obviously a caring and sensitive person who would never want to leave your family financially devastated in the event of your death.

Please stop by my office so I can explain the benefits of life insurance. And because you're my first customer, I can offer you a two-for-one deal.

If you buy one life insurance policy, you can put *two* people on it. That's double the protection for half the price. You can't beat that, Ichabod!

Sincerely,

*Garren Teed*

Garren Teed

P.S. Did you know there's a book called *43 Old Cemetery Road*? I haven't read it, but I hear it's not bad, if you like books. I've never been much of a reader myself.

# IGNATIUS B. GRUMPLY

A WRITER IN RESIDENCE

43 OLD CEMETERY ROAD      2ND FLOOR      GHASTLY, ILLINOIS

July 21

Mr. Garren Teed
We Insure Anything, Inc.
10 Scary Street
Ghastly, Illinois

Dear Mr. Teed,

Not much of a reader indeed. My name is Ignatius B.
Grumply, not *Ichabod B. Grumpy*. And I *am* familiar
with *43 Old Cemetery Road*. I've read the book and can
tell you that it's better than "not bad." In the future, it
would behoove you to do a little research on your potential customers.

You do, however, make a good point about life insurance. I am a sixty-five-year-old man in good health.
I have no plans to die anytime soon. But when I do, I
don't want my son, Seymour, or his mother, Olive, to
worry about money.

Please send me the paperwork for a one-million-dollar
life insurance policy. I do not need a two-for-one policy.
Also, let me know what you find out about tortoise
insurance.

Sincerely,

*Ignatius B. Grumply*

Ignatius B. Grumply

# IGNATIUS B. GRUMPLY

A WRITER IN RESIDENCE

43 OLD CEMETERY ROAD          2ND FLOOR          GHASTLY, ILLINOIS

July 24

Mr. Garren Teed
We Insure Anything, Inc.
10 Scary Street
Ghastly, Illinois

Dear Mr. Teed,

Olive (*not* Olivia) does not *need* life insurance. If you
had read *43 Old Cemetery Road,* you'd know that
Olive is the mother of my son. She's also my writing
partner. Well, sometimes she is. At the moment
we are separated by the Atlantic Ocean. Olive says
I remind her of a tortoise because . . . Oh, never mind.
Just send me the life insurance paperwork and let me
know what you find out about the tortoise policy.

Sincerely,

*Ignatius B. Grumply*

Ignatius B. Grumply

P.S. Do *not* stop by my house again without an invitation. I'm very busy writing new chapters. Rather, I
*will* be busy writing as soon as I mail this letter.

29.

### Chapter One

I was born in 1944 in Chicago. My mother, Neva Grumply, was a librarian. Igor B. Grumply, my father, was a brain surgeon. Despite our last name, our family was quite happy in those days. During the holiday season, we always baked cookies and decorated the house with evergreens. In the spring, we rode bicycles around our neighborhood in Oak Park. In the fall, we picked apples at a nearby orchard. I can still remember the taste of an apple pie my mother baked when I was

*YOU FORGOT SUMMER.*

Olive, is that you? Are you and Seymour back from Scotland already? Good, because that tortoise Seymour borrowed from the library is worth ten thous

*I'M NOT OLIVE. WHAT'S WRONG, IGNATIUS? YOU'RE FROWNING. YOU LOOK JUST LIKE YOU DID WHEN YOU WERE TWELVE.*

Tell me it isn't true.

*IT IS TRUE. IT'S ME, UNCLE IAN.*

Who said you could come to Ghastly? I didn't invite you here.

*WHEN YOU'RE A GHOST, YOU DON'T NEED AN INVITATION.*

Leave! Right now. I demand it.

30.

*I'M SORRY, BUT I CAN'T. I HAVE SOME UNFINISHED BUSINESS WITH YOU.*

What do you mean *unfinished business*?

*I'VE BEEN SENT HERE TO DEBUNK A MYTH.*

Then go back to Scotland. You can debunk the myth of the Loch Ness Monster.

*IT'S SOMETHING ELSE. BUT WE CAN DISCUSS IT LATER. RIGHT NOW I'D LIKE TO GET SETTLED IN. ISN'T THERE A COZY LITTLE APARTMENT ON THE TOP FLOOR?*

That's where Olive lives. Well, she doesn't exactly *live* there. She's dead.

*I KNOW ALL ABOUT OLIVE. I READ YOUR BOOK, REMEMBER? NOW, IF YOU'LL FORGIVE ME, I'LL MAKE MY WAY TO THE CUPOLA. I DON'T SUPPOSE SPENCE MANSION HAS AN ELEVATOR.*

No, it doesn't.

*THAT'S FINE. I USUALLY TAKE STEPS TO AVOID ELEVATORS.*

Uncle Ian, that's a *terrible* joke. You're no funnier in death than you were in life.

*NOT MUCH HAS CHANGED BETWEEN US, HAS IT? I WAS ALWAYS DYING TO MAKE YOU LAUGH.*

Shouldn't you be in a cemetery in Scotland? Well? Shouldn't you? Uncle Ian? Oh, no. He's moving in.

# THE LOCH NESS NEWS

"We cover everything that lurks beneath the headlines"

Saturday, July 25

£1.30

## Rest in Peace, Dr. Ian Grumply

Dr. Ian Grumply was remembered at his memorial service yesterday as a man who loved to laugh.

"Whenever Dr. Grumply came to lunch, he always had a joke to tell," said Carrie N. Haggis, owner of the Loch Ness Café. "He tried to keep everyone laughing. He said the ability to maintain a hearty sense of humor was important, especially during stressful times, like our current economic depression."

Grumply died on July 9 at the age of 103. He spent his professional life practicing psychiatry. His only surviving relatives are his nephew, Ignatius B. Grumply, and his great-nephew, Seymour Hope.

**Ian Grumply loved good jokes and bad puns.**

## Hope Settles in at Grumply Castle

**Hope hasn't decided what to do with Grumply Castle.**

Seymour Hope, the only heir to the estate of the late Dr. Ian Grumply, is the new owner of Grumply Castle, the most valuable piece of real estate on Loch Ness. The 12-year-old American boy arrived at the medieval castle last week from his home in Illinois.

"I can't believe how old this place is," said Hope. "I also can't believe Olive made me wear a skirt to my great-uncle's funeral."

Hope, who is clearly not a fan of kilts, said he hasn't decided what he'll do with Grumply Castle. "My dad thinks I should sell it," said Hope. "But I want to hear what Olive thinks."

**Grumply Castle is nestled on the banks of Loch Ness.**

# Macon Deals Unveils Plans for Loch Vegas

Despite the bleak economy, Macon Deals says he sees a bright future for Loch Ness. The American developer unveiled plans yesterday for a project he's calling Loch Vegas. The plans include a resort with nine swimming pools, seven chocolate fountains and a world-class casino. Local reaction was mixed.

"I can't say I love the idea," said Ben Plaid, owner of the Loch & Key Inn. "But we need something new to bring tourists back to town."

"I disagree," said Carrie N. Haggis, owner of the Loch Ness Café. "Who needs a resort and casino when we have Nessie?"

Nessie is the nickname given to the Loch Ness Monster, a creature that has allegedly lived in Loch Ness for more than 1,500 years. The last reported sighting of the monster was 32 years ago, but the photograph offered as evidence was later proven to be a fake.

Deals says his project will boost the Loch Ness economy by providing jobs for local workers and bringing tourists to town. "Using a monster as a marketing gimmick was cute," said Deals. "But it's been done to death. What Loch Ness needs is Loch Vegas! And I know right where I want to build it."

**Deals says his project will boost local economy.**

Deals refused to specify the property he has in mind for Loch Vegas. "But if you happen to own a large medieval building that sits on the edge of Loch Ness, give me a call," he said. "I'm staying at the Loch & Key Inn."

Testing, one, two. I wonder if my phone works in Scotland.

 I read you loud and clear here in Washington, D.C.

 I didn't know you were listening, Eve Strop.

 I'm always listening, sir. As your director of intelligence, that's my job.

 Yeah, yeah. Now listen to this. I need some help over here in Loch Ness.

 Anything, sir.

 I want bugs in Grumply Castle.

 You mean like ants? Termites? Bedbugs?

 No. On the phones! Bugs. Taps. Whatever you call 'em.

 You want me to tap a landline in Scotland?

 Yeah. Can you do it from there?

It's against the law for private citizens to record the phone calls of others without their permission.

 Blah, blah, blah. If I wanted to obey the law, would I need you?

 Good point, sir.

 I'm trying to build Loch Vegas, and I need Grumply Castle.

 Then buy it.

 I intend to. But I want it at the lowest price.

 And phone taps serve this purpose how?

 By letting me know how much the kid wants for the castle. His dad is back in Illinois. The two are probably discussing the matter right now. So tap the phones and send me transcripts of their conversations.

 Okay. Anything else, sir?

 Find out who Olive is.

July 27

Dear Iggy,

I can't wait to tell you about Grumply Castle! It was built more than five hundred years ago. Back then, the castle was used as a fortress to defend against invading forces. They had a drawbridge to let friends in and keep enemies out. Victories were celebrated in the Great Hall. I can almost picture the grand feasts they had, can't you?

Unfortunately, nobody could agree who owned this castle. People fought for control of it for hundreds of years. Someone even blew up part of the castle to prevent anyone else from having it. (Sheesh!)

Not surprisingly, the castle fell into ruins. People began using it as a quarry. They hauled away stones to build their own homes. That's when your uncle Ian bought this place and renamed it Grumply Castle.

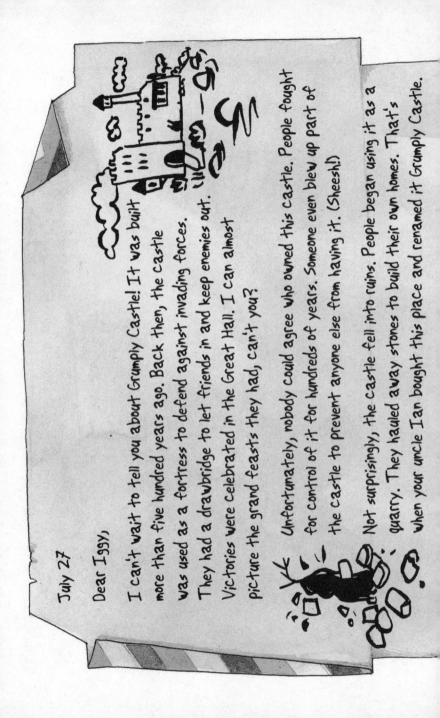

Today, even though much of the castle is destroyed, it's still really cool. Mr. Poe and I are sleeping in a bedroom on the third floor. Olive prefers the privacy of the highest tower. It probably reminds her of the cupola at Spence Mansion.

Olive thinks Grumply Castle would be a fun place to come for vacation every year. She said we could spend our summers looking for Nessie. What do you think, Iggy?

Hope you're having fun writing about your childhood. Please send me a letter when you get a chance.

Miss you,

—Seymour

P.S. Olive still doesn't know I brought Mr. Poe here, so when you write back, don't mention him, okay? He's using Olive's trunk as his bed. I think he likes Scotland.

# IGNATIUS B. GRUMPLY

A WRITER IN RESIDENCE

43 OLD CEMETERY ROAD      2ND FLOOR      GHASTLY, ILLINOIS

August 1

Seymour Hope
43 Old Castle Road
Loch Ness, Scotland

Dear Seymour,

I have no interest in spending my summers in Scotland chasing ludicrous myths about a sea monster. I hope you realize there is *no such thing* as a Loch Ness Monster. Anyone who believes in it is crazy.

Now let me tell you something that *is* true. That tortoise you borrowed from the library is worth ten thousand dollars. I'm trying to buy tortoise insurance, but it's complicated. It would be best if you simply brought back Mr. Poe alive and in one piece. Otherwise, we'll owe the Ghastly Pet Store ten thousand dollars.

I'm not including a note to Olive with this letter. If she asks why, you can tell her I *don't* appreciate being compared to a tortoise.

Love to you,

*Iggy*

P.S. I started work on the new chapters last week but was interrupted. I shall begin writing again in earnest as soon as I post this letter to you.

40.

## 43 OLD CEMETERY ROAD
## GROWING UP GRUMPLY

### Chapter One

I was born in 1944 in Chicago. I had a happy childhood until the age of twelve, when I was forced to begin spending my summers with Uncle Ian. He told terrible jokes, embarrassed me in front of strangers, and was the most ridiculous man who ever lived.

*ANYTHING ELSE YOU DIDN'T LIKE ABOUT ME?*

You were so old.

*I WAS FIFTY THE FIRST SUMMER WE SPENT TOGETHER. THAT'S CONSIDERABLY YOUNGER THAN YOU ARE NOW, IGNATIUS. I WONDER IF SEYMOUR IS EMBARRASSED BY YOUR AGE.*

Of course he's not! I don't *do* the ridiculous things *you* did. Remember all those awful jokes you used to tell? The puns were the worst.

*I THOUGHT JOKES ABOUT GERMAN SAUSAGE WERE THE WURST.*

Really, Uncle Ian. Why?

*WHY WHAT?*

*Why* do you tell such terrible jokes? My father said you were a brilliant psychiatrist. He claimed you were even smarter than he was. But with me, you were always a clown. You made a silly fool of yourself. Why?

*YOU WANT THE HONEST ANSWER?*

41.

Of course I do.

IT WASN'T BECAUSE I WAS SILLY, IGNATIUS. IT WAS BECAUSE <u>YOU</u> WERE SAD. I WAS TRYING TO CHEER YOU UP. YOU WERE SUCH A MISERABLE CHILD AFTER THAT SUMMER VACATION.

I *don't* want to talk about that.

I UNDERSTAND. BUT WHEN YOU'RE READY, I'LL BE HERE.

# ≫THE GHASTLY TIMES≪

Monday, August 3
Cliff Hanger, Editor

"We're Living in Ghastly Times"

50 cents
Afternoon Edition

## Grumply Finds Spence Mansion "Creepy" Without Spence, Hope

Everyone knows Ignatius B. Grumply can get grumpy when he's working on new chapters of his family's bestselling book, *43 Old Cemetery Road*. But the Ghastly author seems unusually grouchy lately.

Yesterday when Grumply was lunching at the Ghastly Gourmand, Shirley U. Jest asked if anything was wrong. Grumply made a surprising announcement.

"Nothing's wrong," he said sharply, "unless you consider the fact that Olive and Seymour are in Scotland and I'm home alone in Spence Mansion, which can be downright creepy, if you want to know the truth."

Jest suggested that Grumply borrow a pet from the Ghastly Public Library to keep him company. "Company?" he replied. "I don't need company with *him* in the house!" Grumply then looked over both shoulders, muttered something unpleasant and shuffled away with his back

**Grumply is even grumpier than usual.**

hunched and shoulders rounded.

"He looked just like a grumpy old tortoise," said Jest.

## Is Borrow-a-Pet Program Going to the Dogs?

**Balm bemoans pet-borrowing program.**

Shirley U. Jest was scratched by a tabby cat she borrowed from the Ghastly Public Library. Fay Tality's favorite slippers were chewed to pieces by a puppy she checked out of the library. Even M. Balm, chief librarian at the Ghastly Public Library, was bitten by a borrowed hedgehog.

*Continued on page 2, column 1*

**BORROW** *Continued from page 1, column 2*

"Partnering with the Ghastly Pet Store seemed like a good idea," said Balm. "But it's turning out to be a disaster."

Last month the Ghastly Public Library joined forces with the Ghastly Pet Store to launch Ghastly's first-ever Borrow-a-Pet Program. Anyone with a valid library card can check out any pet from the Ghastly Pet Store for the summer.

"I underestimated how challenging it would be to manage a collection of animals," said Balm, who moved the pet store inventory into the library.

Balm expressed concern about one pet in particular. "I just hope nothing happens to Mr. Poe before Barry A. Lyve returns."

# Garren Teed Now Offering Pet Insurance

Teed is trying to sell insurance.

In addition to auto, health, home and life insurance, Garren Teed is now offering policies to cover pets.

"I spoke with the folks at the home office in Davenport, Iowa, and talked them into selling pet insurance," said Teed. "I got the idea from Ignacio Z. Gumbo. Did you know he lives in a house with the same address as a famous book?"

Teed said he recalls reading a few books when he was in elementary school. "But I don't have time to read now," he said. "I'm too busy selling insurance— well, trying to sell insurance."

Teed hasn't sold a policy since arriving in Ghastly. "But I'm not worried about making my sales quota," he stated. "In fact, I'm very close to selling my first policy. Do you mind if I add a little shout-out here to Ignacio Z. Gumbo? Ignacio, if you're reading this, please call and let me know when I can stop by your house to get your signature on the life insurance policy. That's all we need to seal the deal."

# IGNATIUS B. GRUMPLY*

### A WRITER IN RESIDENCE

**43 OLD CEMETERY ROAD        2ND FLOOR        GHASTLY, ILLINOIS**

August 4

Mr. Garren Teed
We Insure Anything, Inc.
10 Scary Street
Ghastly, Illinois


Dear Mr. Teed,

I saw your "shout-out" in yesterday's newspaper. If you
are now offering pet insurance, where is the policy I
requested for a tortoise two and a half weeks ago? I'm
also waiting for you to send me the life insurance policy
by mail, as I requested.

To be clear, I want to purchase a life insurance policy
that would benefit my son, Seymour Hope, in the event
of my untimely death. There's no need to mention Olive
on the policy. She and I are no longer speaking.

Sincerely,

*Ignatius B. Grumply*

Ignatius B. Grumply


*Please note correct spelling of my name.

# GARREN TEED
## We Insure Anything, Inc.

August 5

Mr. Ignacio Z. Gumbo
43 Old Cemetery Road
Ghastly, Illinois

Dear Mr. Gumbo,

Okay, so maybe this is none of my business. Maybe
I shouldn't offer personal advice to my favorite customer
(well, my favorite *almost* customer), but I can't help it.
So here goes.

Relationships are *tough,* Ignacio. Getting along with another person is not always easy. In fact, it's hard. It can
seem downright *impossible* at times. I know you and Olivia
are going through a rough patch. But just imagine if something terrible happened to you. Wouldn't you want your son
*and* your wife to be covered by a life insurance policy? Of
course you would, Ignacio. I've never met Olivia, but I know
you love her. I *believe* in you two. So please, let me put
Olivia's name on the policy.

As for the tortoise policy, I'm getting some pushback
from my boss on that. She wants to know how an elderly

# GHASTLY PUBLIC LIBRARY

12 SCARY STREET..........................GHASTLY, ILLINOIS
M. BALM..................................................CHIEF LIBRARIAN

August 8


Ignatius B. Grumply
43 Old Cemetery Road
Ghastly, Illinois


Dear Ignatius,

All I know about Mr. Poe is what I read in the *Ghastly Times*. Here's a clipping from last June.

Mac Awbrah, owner of Ghastly Antiques. Over the years Spence's image has reportedly appeared in an old mirror in the antique shop. Attempts to photograph the image have failed.

"If people want to believe in ghosts, let 'em," continued Awbrah. "I certainly don't."

Nor does Barry A. Lyve, owner of Ghastly Pet Store, where a 197-year-old giant tortoise named Mr. Poe curls its mouth into a sly smile whenever anyone mentions Spence's name.

But at the Ghastly Gourmand, owner Shirley U. Jest has given up baking peach pies.

"I'm told it was Olive's favorite dessert," said Jest. "Now I'm not saying I believe in ghosts. I'm just saying every time I bake a peach pie, the dang thing disappears from the cooling rack. Same with chocolate-chip muffins."

Les and Diane Hope were well aware of the history of Spence Mansion when they purchased the house 12 years ago after it

tortoise could possibly be worth ten thousand dollars. She says the reimbursement rate for a tortoise, turtle, or lizard is $3.69, regardless of age.

If you have any information or documents (receipts, photos, awards) that I can attach to your application for insurance that might justify your request for additional coverage, please send it to me pronto. And hey, why not send some flowers to Mrs. Gumbo today, too?

Sincerely trying to help,

*Garren Teed*

Garren Teed

# IGNATIUS B. GRUMPLY

### A WRITER IN RESIDENCE

August 6

Mr. Garren Teed
We Insure Anything, Inc.
10 Scary Street
Ghastly, Illinois

Dear Mr. Teed:

My name is not Ichabod B. Grumpily. It's not Ichabod B. Grumbles. It's not even Ignacio Z. Gumbo.

My name is *Ignatius B. Grumply*. I will *NOT* buy life insurance from a man who is either unwilling or unable to spell my name correctly. Nor will I send flowers to a woman who is *NOT* my wife. (For your information, the name of the woman who is *not* my wife and with whom I have never discussed, considered, or even pondered marriage is Olive C. Spence.)

I will, however, see what I can find out about the tortoise.

Sincerely frustrated,

*Ignatius B. Grumply*

Ignatius B. Grumply

# IGNATIUS B. GRUMPLY

### A WRITER IN RESIDENCE

August 7

M. Balm
Ghastly Public Library
12 Scary Street
Ghastly, Illinois

Dear Mr. Balm,

I'm about to lose my mind. I'm trying to buy a pet insurance policy to cover Mr. Poe. I know the creat is old, but that fact alone isn't enough to justify a t thousand-dollar policy.

Do you know *why* Mr. Poe is so valuable? If you hav any information, please send it my way.

Sincerely exhausted,

*Ignatius B. Grumply*

Ignatius B. Grumply

Does that help? I'll keep digging through the archives. It's always interesting to read old newspapers. Until I found this article, I'd almost forgotten there was a time not very long ago when folks in Ghastly didn't believe Olive existed. Do you think it's possible that Mr. Poe believed in Olive before the rest of us?

One other thing comes to mind. The name Mr. Poe might refer to Edgar Allan Poe, the famous American writer. He's credited with inventing the detective story and what we now refer to as gothic fiction. But I don't think that has any relevance here.

Yours with a mystery to solve!

M. Balm

Where are the transcripts of phone calls between the kid and his dad?

 Don't have them.

 Why not?

 They write letters.

 You mean old-fashioned snail mail?

 Yep.

 People still do that?

 Not many, but Seymour Hope and his father do.

 Then I need to see their letters.

 It's illegal to read people's mail without their permission.

 Blah, blah, blah. I need to know how much the kid wants for Grumply Castle!

I'll have to aim a satellite camera at the castle and take photos of the letters.

 Do it. What did you find out about Olive?

 Olive is Seymour's mother. She and the boy's father are coauthors of a book titled *43 Old Cemetery Road*.

 Is it any good?

 Dunno. Haven't read it, but millions have.

 What's the gimmick?

 They claim Olive's a ghost.

 And that works?

 It must. The book is an international bestseller.

 Because of a *ghost* gimmick? Interesting. I'm adding Dewey D. Zine to this conversation. Are you there, Dewey?

Yes, sir. I'm here.

 Hi, Dewey.

 Hi, Eve. Nice to meet you.

 You too.

 Less chat, more work. Dewey, listen up. Design a ghost feature for Loch Vegas.

 Yes, sir. Where do you want it? Grumply Castle?

 I don't own the place yet, but I want to move quickly on this ghost gimmick.

 How can we, sir, if we don't have any land to build on? We can't build in the lake.

 Ha! Of course we can! That's brilliant! We'll make it a water slide. The Loch Ness water slide!

 Or you could call it the Ghost of Nessie water slide.

Good idea, Eve.

 It's *my* idea. I own everything we discuss. Now go design it, Dewey.

 I'm fairly certain it's illegal to build a commercial enterprise in a public lake.

 Blah, blah, blah. By the end of the day, I want to see plans for a Ghost of Nessie water slide.

 Yes, sir.

*From the Desk of Dewey D. Zine*
**Senior Designer and Director of Special Projects**
**Macon Deals, Inc.**

## Plans for Ghost of Nessie Water Slide Park

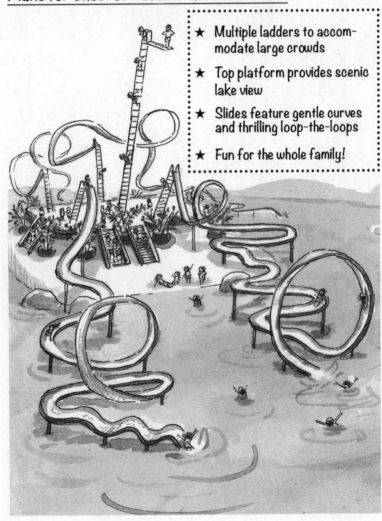

★ Multiple ladders to accommodate large crowds

★ Top platform provides scenic lake view

★ Slides feature gentle curves and thrilling loop-the-loops

★ Fun for the whole family!

# THE LOCH NESS NEWS

"We cover everything that lurks beneath the headlines"
Tuesday, August 11

£1.30

## Deals Will Build Water Slide Park in Loch Ness

If you can't beat 'em, join 'em. That seems to be the logic behind Macon Deals's decision to build a Nessie-themed water slide park in Loch Ness.

"A lot of people still associate this lake with that old monster legend," said Deals at a press conference yesterday. "So it makes sense to build a Ghost of Nessie water slide right here in Loch Ness. It's all part of my plan to revive the local economy."

Not everyone is as optimistic as Deals. Carrie N. Haggis, owner of the Loch Ness Café, is skeptical that a resort, casino or water slide will boost the economy. "The only person who will profit from Loch Vegas is Macon Deals," said Haggis. "Let's just hope he can't find a place to build his monstrosity."

**Deals shows off plans for water slide.**

Deals, who hopes to have Loch Vegas ready for customers by next spring, hasn't bought property yet for the project. Rumor has it he has his eye on Grumply Castle. (See story, next page.)

## Queen Offers Incentive to Boost Tourism

**The queen is worried about Loch Ness.**

The queen of England is so distressed by the downturn in the local economy that she is offering to confer knighthood or damehood on anyone who can bring a thousand tourists to Loch Ness by September 15.

"Being named a knight or dame is one of the highest honors an individual can achieve," said Bea Prawpa, secretary of communications for Buckingham Palace. "Boosting tourism in Loch Ness is a priority for the queen. It's something she would like to encourage and honor."

Don't count on Max Blew winning the

Continued on page 2, column 1

**QUEEN** *Continued from page 1, column 2*

queen's favor. Blew, owner of House of Blews Bagpipes, says he's tried to remain optimistic during the economic depression. "But you'd have to be a darn fool to try to make a living here."

According to Blew, the problem isn't just that fewer tourists are coming to Loch Ness. "The handful of folks who do visit only come to look and laugh at us," said Blew, who plans to close his shop on September 15. "People think we're a bunch of silly goats for hanging on to hope that a monster lives in our loch," he continued. "Frankly, I'm starting to think they're right."

Carrie N. Haggis at the Loch Ness Café disagrees. "There's nothing silly about believing in Nessie. She's part of our history. If we give up on her, we might as well give up on ourselves."

## Loch Ness Café

"Where we still believe in Nessie!"
Carrie N. Haggis

## House of Blews Bagpipes

Max Blew,
former believer

# Hope Holds the Key to Loch Vegas

Hope hasn't decided whether to keep or sell Grumply Castle.

There's no question that Grumply Castle is the most valuable piece of real estate in the Loch Ness region. The question is: Will Seymour Hope sell the ancient castle to Macon Deals, and if so, for how much?

The 12-year-old American boy said he's had little time to consider the matter since arriving in Scotland a month ago. "Olive's been showing me all around Loch Ness," said Hope. "She wants me to see everything she saw when she was here as a 12-year-old girl. She also wants me to find a souvenir to take home so I'll always remember this trip. She said she still has her souvenir from Loch Ness."

When asked if he had spoken with Deals about Grumply Castle, Hope said no. Then he pulled a note from his pocket and read it. "Olive thinks if Mr. Deals wants to buy Grumply Castle, he should write me a letter," said Hope.

THE LOCH & KEY INN
44 TARTAN LANE
LOCH NESS, SCOTLAND

SEYMOUR HOPE
43 OLD CASTLE ROAD
LOCH NESS, SCOTLAND

August 12

Seymour Hope
43 Old Castle Road
Loch Ness, Scotland

Dear Seymour,

So "Olive" thinks I should write you a letter, huh? That's cute, kid. But while you're cracking ghost jokes, the Loch Ness economy is vanishing into thin air. This place is turning into a ghost *town*. Or haven't you noticed the long faces? People here need money. They need *jobs*. I can provide all that with Loch Vegas, but I need Grumply Castle to do it.

So here's my offer: I'll give you five hundred bucks for your castle. That's a lot of money for a kid your age. To sweeten the deal, I'll even throw in a gift certificate for a free weekend at Loch Vegas for your dad.

What do you say? Are you willing to make a deal?

*Macon Deals*

Macon Deals

NEW YORK    LAS VEGAS    LONDON    TOKYO    BERLIN
AND COMING SOON—LOCH VEGAS!

60.

43 Old Castle Road
Loch Ness, Scotland

August 14

Macon Deals
The Loch & Key Inn
44 Tartan Lane
Loch Ness, Scotland

Dear Mr. Deals,

I know you want to buy Grumply Castle. I also know people here need jobs. I'm sorry if I sound selfish, but I don't think I want to sell this cast

There's no need to apologize, dear. Five hundred dollars is an absurd offer.

That's what I thought, Olive. But I don't know anything about property values.

Nor do I. During my life I built only one house, Spence Mansion, and that was in 1874. Prices were much lower back then. But that's beside the point. If you don't want to sell Grumply Castle, you don't have to. I could stay here forever, gazing at the lake and looking for Nessie.

Iggy says only crazy people believe in Nessie.

Oh, he does, does he? Maybe you and I should remain at Grumply Castle and let your father live in Spence Mansion.

But what about our family? What about our book?

We could take a break from all that. I can't think of a good reason to return to Ghastly right away. Can you?

Yeah, I can. I need to tell you something important, Olive. But I don't want to do it in a letter to Macon Deals.

Very well, then. Finish this letter to Mr. Deals and mail it. You and I shall talk later.

Okay. Mr. Deals, I don't want to sell Grumply Castle to you.

Sincerely,

—Seymour and Olive C. Spence

August 15

Seymour Hope
43 Old Castle Road
Loch Ness, Scotland

Dear Seymour,

Look, the ghost thing was cute *once*. But you can take a joke too far. After a while it's like the local yokels and their story about a lake monster. Blah, blah, blah.

Five hundred dollars was my starting offer. I can go as high as a thousand bucks and a free *week* at Loch Vegas for your dad.

What do you say, kid?

*Macon Deals*

Macon Deals

## O.C.S.

**Ghost Writer in Residence**
43 Old Castle Road, The Tower
Loch Ness, Scotland

August 17

Macon Deals
The Loch & Key Inn
44 Tartan Lane
Loch Ness, Scotland

Dear Mr. Deals,

Here's what I say to men who refuse to believe in things they can't see: *Blah, blah, blah, and shame on you.*

Seymour doesn't have to sell you Grumply Castle. He doesn't need the money. And for your information, a gift certificate to Loch Vegas would be wasted on Seymour's father. He's a neophobe who will never come to Scotland.

Don't contact us again.

Olive C. Spence

Dewey, are you there?

 Yes, sir.

 I want the Ghost of Nessie water slide to be sassy. Make it say rude things to people.

 You want a *talking* water slide?

 Just do it, Dewey. It's a marketing gimmick. Let's get this thing up and running now.

 Before the resort and casino?

 Yes! I need to bring tourists to town ASAP so I can become a knight.

 If you do, will we have to call you Sir sir?

Stop eavesdropping, Eve Strop!

 It's my job, sir.

Hi, Eve.

Hi, Dewey. How's it going?

Enough chitchat, you two! Eve, do you still have a camera on the castle?

 Yes, sir.

 I need something to convince the kid to sell Grumply Castle. See any blackmail potential?

 You want to blackmail a kid? That's not legal in any jurisdiction in the world. Plus, it's just not right.

 Do you think I care what's legal or right? I want Grumply Castle, and it's *your* job to provide intel that helps me get what I want.

 Okay, but this kid is pretty clean. He spends most days playing with a tortoise.

 What?

 He brought it from home. According to a letter from his father, the tortoise is worth ten thousand dollars.

 Bingo.

Sir?

 If a kid loses a ten-thousand-dollar tortoise, he'll need ten thousand dollars to replace it. That's when I offer to buy Grumply Castle for exactly that. So steal the tortoise.

 Sorry. That's not in my job description.

 Then Dewey, you do it. Design something to move the tortoise out of the castle without anyone seeing you.

 An unmanned satellite-guided cattle prod would probably do the trick.

 Cool idea, Eve.

 It's *my* idea! I own it. I own everything we discuss, everything you draw, everything you even *think* about. So go design it, Dewey. I want to see plans for a high-tech tortoise prod by the end of the day.

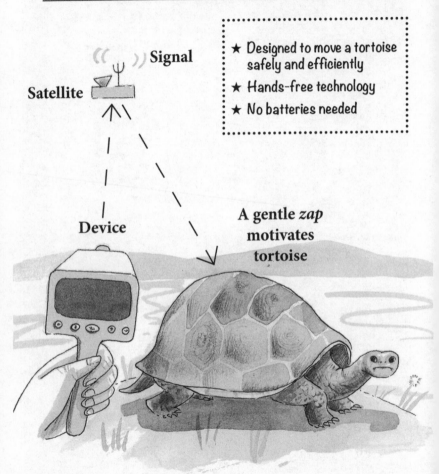

*From the Desk of Dewey D. Zine*
**Senior Designer and Director of Special Projects**
**Macon Deals, Inc.**

## Plans for Satellite-Guided Remote Tortoise Repositioning Device

**Signal**

**Satellite**

- ★ Designed to move a tortoise safely and efficiently
- ★ Hands-free technology
- ★ No batteries needed

**Device**

**A gentle *zap* motivates tortoise**

August 18

The Queen of England
Buckingham Palace
London SW1A 1AA, England


Dear Queen,

First, I want to say hats off—or should I say *crowns* off?—to you for caring about the folks in Loch Ness. As you know, the economy here is really in the dumper, and I can tell you why. They milked that Loch Ness Monster gimmick to *death*. They thought their livelihood depended on getting tourists to believe in an imaginary monster.

But nobody believes in mythical monsters anymore. Nobody's coming to Loch Ness today or tomorrow unless you give people a sparkly new reason to visit. Well, I have just the reason: Loch Vegas, a multimillion-dollar resort and casino—with a water slide! The only problem is, I can't start construction until I purchase and demolish a dilapidated old castle that's currently plopped on the site where I want to build.

So here's what I'm wondering: Would you consider extending your contest deadline by a royal smidgen? I know I can bring a thousand tourists to Loch Ness. I just need a bit more time. What do you say, Queenie?

Sincerely,

*Sir Macon Deals*

Macon Deals

P.S. You can write back to me in care of the Loch & Key Inn.

P.P.S. I don't want to count my chickens before they're hatched, but a knighthood would be totally cool. I'd have to change my stationery and business cards to *Sir Macon Deals,* but that's not a big deal.

**BUCKINGHAM PALACE**
LONDON SW1A 1AA
ENGLAND

August 20

Macon Deals
c/o The Loch & Key Inn
44 Tartan Lane
Loch Ness, Scotland

Dear Mr. Deals,

I regret to inform you that Her Royal Majesty is not interested in moving the contest deadline. Anyone who can bring a thousand tourists to Loch Ness by September 15 of this year will be named a knight or a dame by the Queen.

Also, please be aware that while foreign citizens occasionally do receive honorary knighthoods, they do not then use "Sir" before their names. Hence, there will be no need to change your stationery or business cards in the event that you become a knight.

Yours in service to Her Majesty,

*Bea Prawpa*

Bea Prawpa
Secretary of Communications
Buckingham Palace

Listen up, Dewey. I want the Ghost of Nessie water slide designed, constructed, and open for business *now*.

 But sir, I haven't even found a crew to buil

 Just do it, Dewey! Get over here and build it yourself.

 Yes, sir. Anything else?

 I want the tortoise gone. I don't care where, just get rid of it.

 Repositioning the tortoise in the lake would be the most humane approach.

 Good idea, Eve.

 Whose idea was it?

 Um, it was your idea, sir.

 Now you're talking.

 What happens when the tortoise is successfully relocated?

 We sit back and wait to hear from the kid.

Hawaii became the fiftieth state on August 21, 1959. Nicknamed the Aloha State, Hawaii is a favorite vacation destination for people who enjoy beautiful beaches and tropical rain forests.

Oahu

PM
AUG 24

HAWAII

M. Balm
Ghastly Public
Library
12 Scary Street
Ghastly, Illinois

M. Balm,

Having a great
time in Hawaii.
I'll be home on
September 15.

Barry A. Lyve

P.S. Don't let
anything happen
to Mr. Poe!

# GARREN TEED
## We Insure Anything, Inc.

August 27

Mr. Ignatius B. Grumply
43 Old Cemetery Road
Ghastly, Illinois

Dear Mr. Grumply,

I'm writing with bad news. We can't insure the tortoise for ten thousand dollars. However, I *can* sell you a policy that will pay *six* dollars in the event of tortoise loss or damage. That's the maximum. Do you want me to begin the paperwork?

Speaking of paperwork, I noticed you haven't stopped by my office to pick up your life insurance policy. I have a hunch you and the wife are busy trying to patch things up. No worries! I'm enclosing the policy with this letter. Pretty sure I've got everything spelled correctly this time.

Sincerely,

*Garren Teed*

Garren Teed

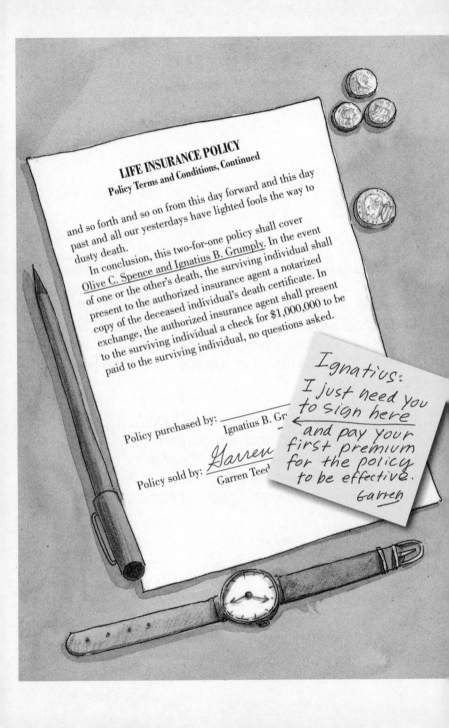

# IGNATIUS B. GRUMPLY

### A WRITER IN RESIDENCE

**43 OLD CEMETERY ROAD**          **2ND FLOOR**          **GHASTLY, ILLINOIS**

August 28

Seymour Hope
43 Old Castle Road
Loch Ness, Scotland

Dear Seymour,

I wasn't able to purchase insurance for Mr. Poe, so please take good care of him. I've done a bit of research on tortoises. They can live more than two hundred years and often go months without food or water. Needless to say, I'm not as worried as I was a few weeks ago. Still, I'll be relieved when I see you walk through the front door of Spence Mansion with a living, breathing tortoise.

Now I must get back to work on the new chapters. I'm having a terrible time writing lately. I think I'd better start from the beginning and type faster.

Love,

*Iggy*

P.S. Has Olive found the Loch Ness Monster yet?
I didn't think so.

## 43 OLD CEMETERY ROAD
## GROWING UP GRUMPLY

### Chapter One

There's an intruder in this house who thinks it's his job to edit my life story. So I must write quickly. Here goes. My childhood was fine until a monster entered my life. His name was Uncle Ian, and he was truly the most awfu

*DO YOU REALLY THINK THAT'S FAIR, IGNATIUS?*

Uncle Ian, you're worse than Olive when it comes to interrupting people! Let me get this straight. You're here because you think we have some unfinished business. Well, you're wrong.

*THEN WHY HAVE YOU NEVER TOLD OLIVE OR SEYMOUR ABOUT YOUR CHILDHOOD?*

Because it's none of their business. It's none of *your* business, either.

*IT'S PRECISELY MY BUSINESS. I WAS A PSYCHIA-TRIST MY ENTIRE PROFESSIONAL LIFE. I'VE BEEN SENT BACK HERE TO HELP YOU DEAL WITH THE SUMMER OF 1956. YOU WERE TWELVE YEARS OLD.*

I've never told *anyone* about that summer. Not even you know the whole story.

*YOU'D NEVER TALK ABOUT IT, IGNATIUS. I KNOW ONLY THE BEGINNING. EVERY SUMMER YOU AND*

**YOUR PARENTS TOOK A VACATION. ONE YEAR YOU WENT TO ARIZONA.**

Because my father wanted to see the Grand Canyon. The next year we went to New York. My mother wanted to see a Broadway show.

**WHERE DID YOU GO THE SUMMER YOU WERE TWELVE?**

Florida.

**WHY?**

Because I wanted to swim in the ocean.

**SO YOU WENT TO FLORIDA WITH YOUR MOTHER AND FATHER. WHAT WAS IT LIKE?**

Hot. Rainy.

**DID YOU GET TO SWIM IN THE OCEAN?**

No. It was raining the day we arrived. My mother said I could swim in the hotel pool. They were offering free swimming lessons.

**CLOSE YOUR EYES AND TELL ME EVERYTHING THAT HAPPENED AT THAT SWIMMING LESSON.**

I *can't* close my eyes and type at the same time! Are you trying to hypnotize me?

THIS IS NOT HYPNOSIS. IT'S PSYCHOTHERAPY. TELL ME EVERYTHING YOU REMEMBER ABOUT THAT DAY.

If I tell you, will you go away?

YES, I PROMISE. NOW TELL ME ABOUT THE SWIMMING LESSON.

All right, but only if this means you'll leave. There were five or six kids in the class. The swimming teacher was a high school girl. I don't remember her name. It was only one lesson.

WHAT DID YOU DO?

We swam, obviously. It was easy. I was already a decent swimmer.

GOOD. HOW LONG DID THE LESSON LAST?

Probably forty-five minutes. Maybe an hour. But I stayed longer.

WHY?

The high dive.

TELL ME ABOUT IT.

At the end of class we were given the option of jumping off the high dive.

**HAD YOU EVER SEEN A HIGH DIVING BOARD?**

Yes, but I'd never jumped off one. I'd always been too scared.

**WHY DID YOU WANT TO TRY IT ON VACATION?**

I don't know. I thought it would be fun. All the kids were doing it.

**TELL ME WHAT HAPPENED.**

I got in line. I stood in the back so I could be last.

**WERE YOU NERVOUS?**

Of course I was nervous! The diving board was thirty feet high. But all the other kids were climbing the ladder and jumping off into the deep end of the pool.

**DID IT LOOK LIKE FUN?**

More scary than fun, but I wanted to do it. My mom and dad were watching. I wanted them to be proud of me.

**WHAT HAPPENED THEN?**

I climbed up the ladder. My legs were shaking. I slowly walked out onto the high dive and . . .

**TELL ME, IGNATIUS. WHAT HAPPENED NEXT?**

Nothing. I couldn't move. I froze.

**YOU WERE FRIGHTENED.**

I was paralyzed with fear.

*I UNDERSTAND. THEN WHAT HAPPENED?*

The swimming teacher was standing below. She said to turn around and climb back down the ladder. But I couldn't.

*WHY NOT?*

I told you! I was *scared*. I curled into a ball. A lifeguard had to carry me down like a baby.

*HOW DID THAT MAKE YOU FEEL?*

How do you *think* it made me feel? Like a fool!

*WHAT HAPPENED AFTER THAT?*

My dad said we had to go home. Our vacation was over.

*I'M SORRY.*

Why are *you* sorry? It was my fault.

*THAT'S NOT TRUE, IGNATIUS.*

It *is* true. I ruined our vacation on the first day. Go ahead, Uncle Ian. Make a joke. Everything is one big joke to you, isn't it?

*NO. BUT NOW I UNDERSTAND WHY YOU WITHDREW INTO YOUR SHELL. NOW WE CAN GET TO WORK.*

# ⟫THE GHASTLY TIMES⟪

Tuesday, September 1
Cliff Hanger, Editor

"We're Living in Ghastly Times"

50 cents
Afternoon Edition

## Librarian Admits Borrow-a-Pet Program Was "Big Mistake"

It was bad enough to be scratched by a cat she borrowed from the Ghastly Public Library. But when Shirley U. Jest came home from work yesterday to find her goldfish missing from its bowl and a contented cat sitting nearby, licking its paws, that was the last straw.

"I returned the cat to the library lickety-split and told Mr. Balm that I had no interest in borrowing another pet," said Jest. "Ever!"

Fay Tality feels equally frustrated. "I thought my borrowed puppy would enjoy playing in the yard while I was at work," she said. "But when I came home yesterday, I discovered that the little beast had spent the day digging up every single rosebush in my garden. I marched that puppy back to the library and told Mr. Balm this was the worst summer library program ever."

M. Balm, chief librarian of the Ghastly Public Library, is hearing many similar complaints. "My phone's been ringing off the hook," he said. "I've heard about bites, scratches, ruined carpets and a monkey who won't stop swinging from a chandelier."

Asked if he planned to offer the Borrow-

**Balm tries to placate cats and catatonic library patrons.**

a-Pet Program next summer, M. Balm said, "Heavens, no. This was a big mistake. I'm just trying to hold on until Barry A. Lyve returns from Hawaii."

Balm said the only good thing about the program is that it's given him a reason to research the history of Ghastly Pet Store. "I found a fascinating story from 1930." (See article on next page.)

**From the Archives of *The Ghastly Times***

# Ghastly Pet Store Celebrates 100th Anniversary

Ever since the dramatic crash on Wall Street last October, many businesses across the United States have been forced to close their doors. But one local business has been able to stay afloat during the current economic downturn.

Ghastly Pet Store, located at 2 Scary Street, is celebrating its 100th anniversary this year. Owner Ari A. Lyve says he considers himself lucky to be able to work in a profession he loves.

"I've always had a fondness for animals," said Lyve. "My great-grandfather was the same way."

According to Lyve, his great-grandfather opened the store in 1830 almost by accident. "Everyone in Ghastly

**Ari A. Lyve is a fourth-generation pet store owner.**

knew my great-granddad loved animals. So whenever anyone found a stray dog or a baby bird that had fallen from its nest, it was brought to my granddad. He cared for any animal, large or small."

Ari A. Lyve continues that tradition today, providing people with pets and pets with homes.

# Garren Teed Hopes to Make Sales Quota

Insurance agent Garren Teed doesn't give up easily. But he admits he's a bit concerned about making his sales quota for the summer.

"The folks at the We Insure Anything home office in Davenport, Iowa, say I have to make five sales before September 15," said Teed. "The good news is, I'm really close to selling a two-for-one policy to Ignatius B. Grumply. I'm hoping that'll count as two sales. So now I just need three more sales, assuming Mr. Grumply signs his policy and returns it to me. Say, if you're reading this, Mr. Grumply, please sign that policy and return it to me as soon as you can, okay?"

**Teed needs to sell at least five policies to keep his job.**

September 4

Dear Iggy,

He's gone. I don't know how or why, but Mr. Poe is gone!

When I went to bed last night, Mr. Poe was sleeping in Olive's old trunk, just like he's done since we left home. But when I woke up this morning, the trunk was empty.

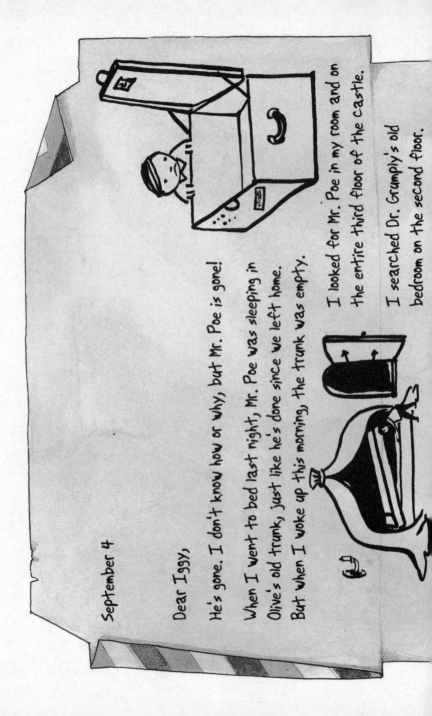

I looked for Mr. Poe in my room and on the entire third floor of the castle.

I searched Dr. Grumply's old bedroom on the second floor.

I looked around the Grand
Hall and up in the tower.

I combed the castle gardens.

I even tried the drawbridge.

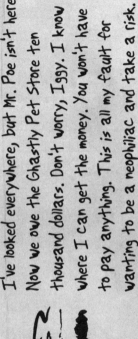

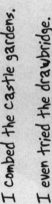

I've looked everywhere, but Mr. Poe isn't here.
Now we owe the Ghastly Pet Store ten
thousand dollars. Don't worry, Iggy. I know
where I can get the money. You won't have
to pay anything. This is all my fault for
wanting to be a neophiliac and take a risk.

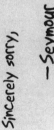

Sincerely sorry,

—Seymour

## LOCH & KEY INN

DATE _Sept. 4_ HOUR _2 p.m._
TO _Macon Deals_

# WHILE YOU WERE OUT

M r. _Seymour Hope_
OF _Grumply Castle_
PHONE _____

❏ Telephoned ❏ Returned Call ❏ Left Package
❏ Please Call ☒ Was In ❏ Please See Me
❏ Will Call Again ❏ Won't Call ☒ Important

MESSAGE: _Seymour Hope stopped by._
_He said he's ready to talk about_
_Grumply Castle._

Signed _Ben Plaid_

# THE LOCH NESS NEWS

### "We cover everything that lurks beneath the headlines"

Saturday, September 5

£1.30

# SOLD!
## Grumply Castle Will Be Demolished

Macon Deals is one step closer to building Loch Vegas now that Seymour Hope has agreed to sell Grumply Castle for ten thousand dollars.

"The kid drove a hard bargain," said Deals. "I'm paying more than I wanted to for that castle, but I'm happy to do it for the future of Loch Ness."

Deals has a bulldozer on site, ready to demolish Grumply Castle so he can build Loch Vegas in its place. But first, he and Hope must officially close the deal on Grumply Castle. "There's a bunch of paperwork we have to sign," said Deals. "My lawyers in New York are working on that right now. But we can still celebrate next Saturday night." (See story below.)

For his part, Seymour Hope said he

**Hope agrees to sell castle to Deals.**

plans to return to the United States as soon as he signs the legal papers. "I'm ready to go home," said Hope hopelessly.

## Water Slide Park to Open Next Saturday Night

Macon Deals is inviting the public to the banks of Loch Ness next Saturday night to celebrate the opening of the Ghost of Nessie water slide park.

"My chief designer, Dewey D. Zine, is here building the main water slide right now," said Deals. "Just wait till you see it. It's thirty feet tall and says sassy things to people as they walk by. It's going to be a tourist magnet!"

Deals said he will take the inaugural trip down the Ghost of Nessie water slide on September 12 at the stroke of midnight. He expects more than a thousand spectators will be on hand to watch.

**Zine updates Deals on project.**

# Village Divided Over Loch Vegas

A heated discussion about the future of Loch Ness took place yesterday afternoon at the Loch Ness Café.

To Carrie N. Haggis, owner of the café, it's a question of pride. "Our parents and grandparents took pride in Nessie," said Haggis. "She was part of our history. Are we going to stand by and watch as someone turns her into a joke by building a Nessie-themed water slide?" Haggis is also troubled by news that Macon Deals plans to demolish Grumply Castle. "It would be a tragedy to tear down that castle," she said.

"I agree it's unfortunate," said Ben Plaid, owner of the Loch & Key Inn. "But what choice do we have? If we want tourists to come back to Loch Ness, we have to give them something to see and do. I've read Macon Deals's business plan. It says more than 10,000 tourists will come here the first year Loch Vegas is open. More than 20,000 will come the second year. And in the third year, more than 30,000 people will come and—"

**Locals discuss Deals's plans and promises.**

"And you believe that?" interrupted Carrie N. Haggis.

"It's better than believing in an imaginary lake monster," observed Max Blew, owner of House of Blews Bagpipes. Blew's shop is scheduled to close on September 15. "I wish I could hold on till Loch Vegas opens," Blew said. "But I haven't sold a bagpipe in years."

# MACON DEALS

## HOTELS ★ RESORTS ★ CASINOS ★ THEME PARKS

September 7

*OVERNIGHT MAIL*

Bea Prawpa
Secretary of Communications
Buckingham Palace
London SW1A 1AA, England

Dear Bea,

Good news! The local newspaper is reporting that at least a thousand tourists will be in Loch Ness on September 12 for the opening of the Ghost of Nessie water slide park, also known as phase one of my Loch Vegas development.

I'd love to get the Queen here for publicity photos. I'm willing to give her a free ticket for a spin down the water slide (after me, of course). While she's in town, the Queen could also make me a knight, thereby saving on gas and royal whatnot. Just trying to be helpful!

Sincerely,

*Macon Deals*

Macon Deals

**NEW YORK     LAS VEGAS     LONDON     TOKYO     BERLIN
AND COMING SOON—LOCH VEGAS!**

## BUCKINGHAM PALACE
### LONDON SW1A 1AA
#### ENGLAND

September 8

Mr. Macon Deals
c/o The Loch & Key Inn
44 Tartan Lane
Loch Ness, Scotland

Dear Mr. Deals,

Her Royal Majesty does not desire to take a "spin" down your
water slide. She will, however, send a representative to Loch Ness
on September 12 to evaluate your efforts to boost tourism.

Yours in service to Her Royal Majesty,

*Bea Prawpa*

Bea Prawpa
Secretary of Communications
Buckingham Palace

September 10

Dear Ignatius,

Are you sitting down?
If not, please do.

I know why Mr. Poe is
worth ten thousand dollars.
I just found an article in the
*Ghastly Times*. It's from
1830. Have a look.

Ignatius, is this mystery
becoming as clear to you
as it is to me?

Sincerely,

M.Balm

M. Balm

## Tortoise Moves to New Home

**Local girl takes tortoise for a walk.**

It was with great sadness that Olive C. Spence, a 12-year-old Ghastly girl, walked a tortoise she found on her summer vacation down Scary Street to Ghastly Pet Store, where she surrendered the creature to the store owner.

"I promise I'll visit Mr. Poe as often as I can," said Olive, who named the tortoise after Mr. Edgar Allan Poe, a talented writer who, as a child, attended school for a brief time in Scotland.

Though charmed by their daughter's interest in nature and literature, Mr. and Mrs. Spence agreed that a giant tortoise is an exotic creature that requires professional care. Hence their decision to ask their daughter to relinquish care of the tortoise to the new pet store.

# IGNATIUS B. GRUMPLY

### A WRITER IN RESIDENCE

43 OLD CEMETERY ROAD       2ND FLOOR       GHASTLY, ILLINOIS

September 11

Mr. M. Balm
Ghastly Public Library
12 Scary Street
Ghastly, Illinois


Dear M. Balm,

*Clear,* Mr. Balm? To me, this whole thing is as clear
as *mud.* I'll give the article another look after I finish
writing for the day. These new chapters are proving
quite difficult for me in more ways than one.


Sincerely,

*Ignatius B. Grumply*

Ignatius B. Grumply

### Chapter One

I was born in 1944. Everything in my life was fine until our disastrous family vacation in Florida. After that, I had to spend every summer with my uncle Ian.

*BACK UP A MINUTE. WHY DO YOU THINK THAT VACATION WAS A DISASTER?*

I already told you. I ruined it when I chickened out of jumping off the high dive. Immediately after that, my parents told me to pack my bags. We went home several days ahead of schedule.

*WHAT IF I TOLD YOU THAT VACATION ENDED EARLY FOR A DIFFERENT REASON?*

There was no other reason. My parents were ashamed.

*WHAT DO YOU REMEMBER ABOUT THE DRIVE BACK TO CHICAGO?*

My parents barely spoke a word.

*BECAUSE THEY WERE WORRIED, IGNATIUS. IT HAD NOTHING TO DO WITH YOU.*

What do you mean?

*HURRICANE BETSY. IT WAS MOVING TOWARD FLORIDA THE DAY YOU ARRIVED. REMEMBER*

THE RAIN? THEY KNEW IT WASN'T SAFE TO STAY
WHERE YOU WERE. SO YOU LEFT FLORIDA EARLY.

*What?* I don't believe this. Why didn't they tell me?

THEY DIDN'T WANT TO WORRY YOU. YOU WERE
ALREADY UPSET ABOUT THE DIVING BOARD INCI-
DENT. WHEN YOU RETURNED HOME, YOU BECAME
ANGRY AND WITHDRAWN. YOU WOULDN'T TALK TO
ANYONE. THAT'S WHY THEY SENT YOU TO ME.

To try to *help* me?

YES. I'M AFRAID I DIDN'T DO A VERY GOOD JOB.

Because I wouldn't talk to you.

YOU WERE ANGRY. BUT IT'S IMPORTANT TO KNOW
THAT ANGER IS A SECONDARY EMOTION.

What does that mean?

WE ALWAYS FEEL SOMETHING ELSE BEFORE WE
FEEL ANGRY. DO YOU REMEMBER HOW YOU FELT
IMMEDIATELY AFTER YOU WERE CARRIED DOWN
FROM THE HIGH DIVE?

Humiliated. Embarrassed. Ashamed.

ANGER IS OFTEN TRIGGERED BY FEAR AND
SHAME. IF YOU COULD CONQUER YOUR FEELINGS
OF SHAME, YOU MIGHT FIND YOURSELF FEELING
LESS ANGRY AT THE WORLD. MAYBE A LITTLE

LESS GRUMPY, TOO. YOU MIGHT EVEN BE ABLE
TO CONQUER YOUR FEAR OF TRYING NEW THINGS.
I SUSPECT YOU ASSOCIATE NEW EXPERIENCES
WITH THAT HIGH DIVE IN FLORIDA.

Are you analyzing me, Uncle Ian?

JUST A BIT. BUT ISN'T IT REMARKABLE HOW
A SEEMINGLY SMALL TRAUMA CAN GROW INTO
SOMETHING MUCH LARGER IF IT'S KEPT SECRET?
DOES THIS MAKE SENSE TO YOU, IGNATIUS?

Yes. It's surprisingly helpful. Thank you.

IF YOU WANT TO THANK ME, TELL OLIVE AND
SEYMOUR ABOUT YOUR PAST.

I will. I'll write them a letter.

NO. TELL THEM IN PERSON. THERE'S A FLIGHT TO
SCOTLAND AT SIX O'CLOCK IN THE MORNING.

Tomorrow?

TAKE A RISK, IGNATIUS. TRY SOMETHING NEW
FOR A CHANGE. FORTUNE FAVORS THE BOLD.

Now you sound like Olive.

I'D LIKE TO MEET THAT GAL.

Then come with me to Scotland.

HA! OKAY. I'LL MEET YOU THERE.

# HEIR AIRLINES

Grumply/Ignatius B.

BOARDING PASS

Sept. 12

**440**
FROM Ghastly, IL (GAS)
TO Loch Ness, Scotland (NSY)

GATE 3 BOARDS AT 5:30 AM

SEAT **21A**

CONFIRMATION NBR J6660C
037 2458373621 CPN 1
037 2458373621 CPN 1
ISSUED BY U201999 AT FFDF47 PHXGS

SEATING

**2**

TKT

Grumply/Ignatius B.

**440**
FROM Ghastly, IL (GAS)
TO Loch Ness, Scotland (NSY)

GATE 3 DEPARTS AT 6:00 AM
ARRIVES AT 8:25 PM

SEAT **21A**

Y-CABIN
037 2458373621 CPN-1

Seymour Hope
43 Old Castle Road
Loch Ness, Scotland
USA
INTERNATIONAL AIRMAIL
Ignatius B. Grumply
43 Old Cemetery Road
Ghastly, Illinois
USA
AEROGRAM

September 12

Dear Iggy,

The weather here is terrible.
It's pouring rain. Mr. Poe is still gone.
I have no idea where he is. I'm sorry
I lost him. I'm sorry you and Olive are fighting.
Everything is my fault. I don't even have the
ten thousand dollars yet. We're still waiting for
the lawyers in New York to send the paperwork.
I don't know what to do except keep looking
for Mr. Poe and . . . .

There's a canoe on the banks of Loch Ness. I don't care how bad the weather is. I'm going in the lake. I'm going to save Mr. Poe.

Wish me luck!

—Seymour

Oh my gosh! I just looked out the window. There's something in the lake.

Could that be Mr. Poe?

Where are you, Dewey?

 I'm making the final adjustments to the water slide.

 Good. I'm at the Loch & Key. I can be on the slide in two minutes.

 It's only 11:45. You said you were going to take the first slide at midnight.

 What have I told you about eavesdropping, Eve?

 Just trying to help, sir.

 Waiting might be a good idea. The fog is terrible now.

 Thick as pea soup.

 Who's that?

 Your favorite gimmick.

Dewey, I don't want the water slide saying sassy things to *me*!

 It's not the slide, sir.

 Then what is it?

 It's *me*.

 Whoever you are, it's against the law to read other people's private messages without their permission.

 Then you're in a world of trouble.

 Eve, is that you?

 No, sir. The message is coming from the edge of the lake.

 Then turn on the satellite camera and tell me who it is!

 All I see is a pair of opera glasses.

 Forget it. It's 11:47. I'm leaving the Loch & Key now. I'll be at the Ghost of Nessie water slide at the stroke of midnight.

Sir, there's an old man on the water slide. He's climbing the ladder.

 *What?* It's *my* water slide. I'm supposed to slide down it first! I bet it's the Queen's representative.

 Does the Queen's representative have a receding hairline and a face like a turtle?

 Good heavens. That sounds like Iggy. When did he get here?

 Just in time, it seems.

 Dr. Grumply, is that you? I was hoping to make your acquaintance.

 Likewise, Miss Spence.

 Turtle Guy's almost to the top of the slide.

 Stop him! Nobody goes down my water slide before me!

Now the turtle guy is holding his nose. Looks like he's ready to go.

 Dewey, dismantle the slide! Tear it down!

 You want me to demolish the water slide I just built?

 Destroying a water slide in a public space with an old man on top and hundreds of spectators nearby is surely in violation of local public safety ordinances.

 Gosh, you're smart, Eve.

 Thanks, Dewey.

 It might be fun to meet in person sometime.

 Really? I was thinking the same thi

 WOULD YOU TWO STOP MAKING SMALL TALK? Forget it. I'll tear down the water slide myself. Are the keys in the bulldozer?

Yes, but it's hard to see in this fog.

 Blah, blah, blah. [Sound of engine starting] Wow, this dozer is a snap to start. Here goes!

 I really think you should stop, sir. I don't think you realize how close you are to the edge of the la

[Sound of loud SPLASH as bulldozer crashes into slide and capsizes into lake]

 Look! Turtle Guy just jumped from the top of the water slide.

[Sound of quieter SPLASH as elderly writer jumps into lake]

 Good boy!

 Why would Iggy jump from the top of a thirty-foot water slide? I don't under-stand any of this. Oh, dear, and look how he's splashing about. I'd better help him.

[Sound of faint SPLASH as opera glasses hit water]

I bet I'm out of a job now.

 Same here. Want to keep in touch?

 Definitely. Maybe we could meet for coffee or lunch or even dinn

 Dewey, I'm sorry to interrupt, but do you see what I see in the middle of the lake? Long neck. Small head. Three humps. It must be something funny with the satellite camera.

 Wait, I see it, too. You don't think it could be . . . Or could it?

 It is! It's . . . it's . . . it's . . .

# THE LOCH NESS NEWS

**"We cover everything that lurks beneath the headlines"**

Sunday, September 13

£2

---

# *NESSIE?*

**This three-humped creature with glasses appears to be Nessie.**

Nearly a thousand people came to Loch Ness last night to watch Macon Deals slide down the brand-new Ghost of Nessie water slide. What many say they saw instead was the Loch Ness Monster.

"I knew Nessie wouldn't let us down!" said Carrie N. Haggis, owner of the Loch Ness Café. "Just when everybody was ready to give up on her, Nessie made a surprise appearance."

"I predict we're going to see a lot of tourists because of this," said Ben Plaid, owner of the Loch & Key Inn. "I'm already getting phone calls from people all over the world who want to make reservations. Everyone wants to come visit Loch Ness and look for Nessie."

That's good news for local shop owners, including Max Blew, owner of House of Blews Bagpipes. "I sold three sets of bagpipes this morning," said Blew with a big smile. "I guess I could keep the shop open a little while longer."

The only person in Loch Ness who wasn't smiling after last night's sighting was Macon Deals. (See story below.)

## Not a Good Knight for Macon Deals

Macon Deals has some explaining to do. So says Bea Prawpa, secretary of communications to Her Royal Majesty. "When I told the queen about Mr. Deals's plans to demolish Grumply Castle, she was very upset," said Prawpa, who was sent by Queen Elizabeth to investigate Deals. "I couldn't believe my eyes when I saw Macon Deals driving a bulldozer like a madman through a crowd of people. I immediately called Her Majesty, who got on the royal horn to Scotland Yard."

Within minutes of Prawpa's call, police arrived and arrested Deals. "We charged him with reckless endangerment of a

*Continued on page 2, column 1*

**KNIGHT** *Continued from page 1, column 2*
village and a tortoise," said officer Sue Pina. Deals then surrendered his phone, which Pina said contained many incriminating messages. "Scotland Yard is now launching a full-blown investigation into Macon Deals's business practices."

"He didn't even bring a thousand tourists to town," added Prawpa. "There were exactly 907. I counted."

Deals, who had hoped to be named a knight last night, instead was taken to the Loch Ness jail after being rescued from a bulldozer submerged in Loch Ness.

Macon Deals makes poor impression on Bea Prawpa.

# Father, Son and Tortoise Reunited

The tortoise and the heir join Grumply after lake scare.

While most eyes were on Nessie, another adventure was unfolding in Loch Ness shortly after midnight. Seymour Hope, the 12-year-old American heir to Grumply Castle, was trying to rescue a giant tortoise.

"I saw Mr. Poe in the lake," said Hope. "So I got in a canoe and tried to row out to get him, but the canoe overturned. Luckily Iggy was right there when I needed him."

Iggy is Hope's nickname for his father, Ignatius B. Grumply, who arrived in Loch Ness last night. When told by onlookers that his son was in the lake, Grumply jumped from the top of the Ghost of Nessie water slide and then swam through the cold, choppy water to save his son and the giant tortoise.

Father, son and tortoise are now resting comfortably in Grumply Castle, which is still Hope's property. "I never signed the final paperwork with Macon Deals," said Hope happily.

"Told you so!"
Carrie N. Haggis

# SEYMOUR HOPE
### Illustrator in Residence

43 Old Castle Road
Third floor
Loch Ness, Scotland

September 13

Dear Olive and Iggy,

I can't believe you both jumped into Loch Ness to rescue me and Mr. Poe!

Olive's glasses

Iggy's foot

My head

Mr. Poe's shell

The overturned canoe

When you put it all together in the fog, I can see why people thought we were Nessie.

112.

Macon Deals certainly did. I'm glad we scared that monster away.

Me too! I'm even happier we found Mr. Poe. I'm really sorry I didn't tell you I brought him with us on vacation. But now we can take him home and we won't have to pay the Ghastly Pet Store ten thousand dollars. Can you believe that's how much he's worth?

Yes, I can. But Mr. Poe needs to stay here.

Olive, how can you say that?

Because Loch Ness is his home. When I was your age, I brought Mr. Poe to Ghastly. He was my souvenir from Scotland. I hid him in my trunk. Those holes you thought you were lucky to find in my old steamer trunk were holes I made in 1830 on my voyage home from Scotland.

What? Then how did Mr. Poe get to the Ghastly Pet Store?

My parents wouldn't let me keep him. They insisted I donate him to the new pet store and let a professional care for him.

And Mr. Poe's been living at the Ghastly Pet Store ever since?

That's right. I visited him daily for years. But Mr. Poe's getting old. I've known for a while that he wanted to come home. He was too heavy for me to carry. I was hoping you might hide him in my trunk and bring him back here.

Olive, you knew???

Of course I knew. But I didn't mind. I wanted Mr. Poe to come home. Just look at him smile. He must be so happy to be back in the land of the Loch Ness Monster.

Did you hear that? Mr. Poe laughed when you wrote Loch Ness Monster. There! He did it again!

Good heavens. How odd.

Olive, do you think Mr. Poe saw the Loch Ness Monster last night?

Look! He's laughing again. He laughs every time we write the words *Loch Ness Monster.*

Is it possible Mr. Poe knew the Loch Ness Monster when he was young? Do you think they might've been friends or maybe even family? Do you think there will be more real sightings of Nessie now that Mr. Poe is back?

It's possible, Seymour. Anything's possible. I don't care if you grow up to be a neophobe or a neophiliac. Just promise me you'll be someone who believes *anything* is possible.

I will, Olive. Wow! This moment is the best souvenir of Scotland I could ever wish for. I can't wait to tell Iggy about Mr. Poe!

Run and tell him now. I need to write a letter.

## O.C.S.

Ghost Writer in Residence
43 Old Castle Road, The Tower
Loch Ness, Scotland

September 13

Ignatius B. Grumply
43 Old Castle Road, Second Floor
Loch Ness, Scotland


Dear Iggy,

I don't think I've ever been prouder of you than I was last night when I watched you jump into Loch Ness and save Seymour. I know you didn't want to come to Scotland, but I'm so glad you did. You are the bravest man I know.

Meanwhile, I am the least courageous ghost who's ever haunted this earth. I apologize for not telling you my real reason for wanting to come to Scotland. I should've brought Mr. Poe back decades ago and set him free. But it's strange, Iggy. The older I get, the harder it is to let go of childhood things, even a pet tortoise.

In any case, I shall pay the Ghastly Pet Store ten thousand dollars. I have some money tucked away in the cupola for emergencies. I don't want to burden you or Seymour with this expense.

Sincerely ready to go home,

Olive

# IGNATIUS B. GRUMPLY

## A WRITER IN RESIDENCE

**43 OLD CASTLE ROAD**         **2ND FLOOR**         **LOCH NESS, SCOTLAND**

September 13

Olive C. Spence
The Tower
43 Old Castle Road
Loch Ness, Scotland

Dear Olive,

We have plenty of money in our bank account to pay the Ghastly Pet Store ten thousand dollars. I'm not worried about that. But I do want to apologize for not coming to Scotland with you and Seymour in the first place. As it turns out, I had some unfinished business to take care of with Uncle Ian. Like you, I had something from my childhood that I needed to set free. I'd like to tell you and Seymour about it later today.

Oh, good. I'm so glad we're talking again, dear. How do you like Grumply Castle?

It's quite a place. We should come here every summer for vacation.

I agree! I only wish we'd come here when your uncle was still alive. We could've had some laughs together in Grumply Castle.

Olive, that's it!

What?

Think about it. If you're allowed to stay around as a
ghost and write books, why couldn't Uncle Ian stay here
in Grumply Castle to work on his research? We could
turn the castle into a center dedicated to the study of
humor. It could also be the official home of Mr. Poe, the
laughing tortoise.

Iggy, that's a brilliant idea. People would come
for miles to see a tortoise laugh. Doctors could
study the healing power of humor. Children
could learn how to write good jokes and bad puns.

People like me could come and exercise our funny bones.

Exactly! It would be wonderful for the local
economy. We have to talk to Seymour about it.
It's his castle. But I bet he'll love the idea. Let's
have a meeting in an hour. We'll need to discuss
how to make a few tasteful modifications to the
castle. We shouldn't do anything that detracts
from its grandeur, but we'll want our guests to be
comfortable. Oh, and let's make sure it's free, too.
Do we have enough money in our bank account
for that? We'll need a million dollars to do this
right. What's wrong, Iggy? You have the strang-
est look on your face.

Olive, do you by any chance have a death certificate?

Of course. Everyone who dies gets one.

Good. Let's talk to Seymour. Then let's all go home.
There's something on my desk I need to sign.

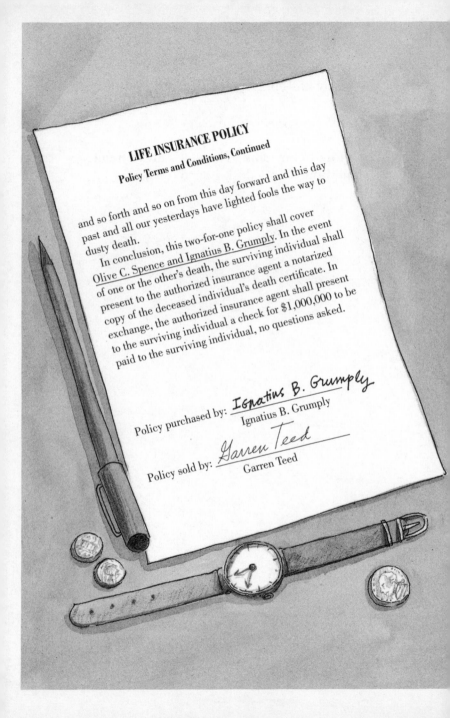

### LIFE INSURANCE POLICY

#### Policy Terms and Conditions, Continued

and so forth and so on from this day forward and this day past and all our yesterdays have lighted fools the way to dusty death.

In conclusion, this two-for-one policy shall cover <u>Olive C. Spence and Ignatius B. Grumply</u>. In the event of one or the other's death, the surviving individual shall present to the authorized insurance agent a notarized copy of the deceased individual's death certificate. In exchange, the authorized insurance agent shall present to the surviving individual a check for $1,000,000 to be paid to the surviving individual, no questions asked.

Policy purchased by: <u>*Ignatius B. Grumply*</u>
Ignatius B. Grumply

Policy sold by: <u>*Garren Teed*</u>
Garren Teed

# ➤THE GHASTLY TIMES◄

Tuesday, September 15
Cliff Hanger, Editor

"We're Living in Ghastly Times"

50 cents
Afternoon Edition

## Ghastly's Favorite Family Returns with Plans for Loch Ness Laughitorium

**The talented trio plans to renovate Grumply Castle.**

**Mr. Poe, the laughing tortoise, will remain in Scotland.**

Ignatius B. Grumply and Olive C. Spence returned home to Spence Mansion last night with their son, Seymour Hope, and a million-dollar plan.

"We're going to turn Grumply Castle into a laughitorium," said Seymour Hope. "The official name will be the Loch Ness Laughitorium, Home of Mr. Poe, the Laughing Tortoise."

Ignatius B. Grumply explained the concept. "We want Grumply Castle to be a place where people can go whenever they need a good laugh," he said. "We also want doctors to continue my brilliant uncle Ian's research into the healing power of humor."

The renovated castle will feature comfortable guest rooms, a library filled with funny books and classrooms for cartooning and joke writing.

The million-dollar renovation will be funded by an insurance claim paid to Grumply by Garren Teed. (See story on next page.)

# Borrow-a-Pet Program Ends with a Promise

The disastrous Borrow-a-Pet program ended today with the return of Barry A. Lyve, the owner of Ghastly Pet Store. Lyve, who returned from Hawaii this morning, apologized for the borrowed pets' poor behavior. "For many of these animals, the pet store is the only home they've ever known. It's hard to be separated from friends and family. I think that's why some of the pets were acting up."

To compensate for the inconvenience, Lyve is donating the $10,000 he received from the Grumply-Spence-Hope family to the Ghastly Public Library. Balm already knows how he wants to spend it.

"Would anyone like me to use the money to charter a plane to Scotland next summer to visit Mr. Poe at the Loch Ness Laughitorium?" Balm asked a group of library patrons.

"Sign me up for that!" said Shirley U. Jest.

**Barry A. Lyve signs over check to M. Balm.**

"Count me in," said Fay Tality.

"Me too," added Barry A. Lyve, who had no idea the giant tortoise was originally from Scotland and was at one time Olive C. Spence's pet. "Now I know why Mr. Poe always smiled whenever anyone mentioned her name."

# Garren Teed Loses One Job, Finds Another

Garren Teed sold only one insurance policy in Ghastly. But it was a doozie.

"The home office in Davenport said they'd never had to pay out a million-dollar claim the same day a policy was signed," said Teed, who was fired from We Insure Anything earlier today.

"That's what happens when you don't read books," said Ignatius B. Grumply, who purchased the two-for-one policy from Teed. "If Mr. Teed had read just a few pages of *43 Old Cemetery Road,* he would've known that Olive has been dead since 1911."

Grumply laughed and said Garren Teed wasn't a bad fellow. "He was just in the wrong business." Grumply then presented Teed with a one-way ticket to Scotland. "We need someone in Loch Ness to feed

**Garren Teed will no longer sell insurance.**

a tortoise and oversee the renovation of Grumply Castle," he said. "Mr. Teed won't have to sell a thing. He might even have time to read a book or two."

# New Chapters Will Be Called "The Loch Ness Punster"

Three new chapters of the bestselling book *43 Old Cemetery Road* are almost finished and ready to be mailed to subscribers.

"I was planning to call the new chapters 'Growing Up Grumply,'" said Ignatius B. Grumply. But when he started writing about his childhood, Grumply said he discovered a more interesting story. "My uncle Ian was a fascinating man. He told terrible jokes and puns, but I finally know why. I just wish I'd listened to him earlier. Maybe I wouldn't have spent so many years being grumpy."

Grumply said the new chapters, which he's calling 'The Loch Ness Punster,' will include the story of his family's recent vacation to Scotland and a mon-

**Grumply is almost finished with new chapters.**

ster they met at Loch Ness. "His name is Macon Deals, but I'll let Olive and Seymour tell that part."

**Chapter One**

When I was twelve, I began spending my summers with my uncle, Dr. Ian Grumply. Back then, I didn't like his terrible jokes or bad puns. But now I see what a brilliant man Uncle Ian was and still is. He helped me debunk a myth from my childhood. For that I want to say thank you from the bottom of my

*STOP. YOU'RE EMBARRASSING ME.*

Ha! You're back in Ghastly!

*I AM. AND I SEE I MADE YOU LAUGH—FINALLY.*

Thank you, Uncle Ian, for everything.

*YOU'RE WELCOME, IGNATIUS. AND WE MIGHT AS WELL SAY GOODBYE NOW. I WON'T BE ABLE TO STICK AROUND MUCH LONGER.*

Aren't you going back to Scotland? I thought you'd want to continue your humor research. That was the whole point of turning the castle into a laughitorium.

*IT'S A WONDERFUL IDEA, BUT OTHERS CAN FINISH WHAT I STARTED. MY UNFINISHED BUSINESS WAS WITH YOU.*

I understand. I'm so lucky to have had you as my uncle. Or should I say I'm *lochy*?

124.

*WHERE DID YOU GET SUCH A <u>PUNNY</u> SENSE OF HUMOR?*

From you, of course.

*THAT MAKES ME SMILE. GOODBYE, IGNATIUS.*

Goodbye, Uncle Ian. Wait! Don't go yet. I have one more question.

*ASK QUICKLY. I CAN FEEL MYSELF BEING PULLED AWAY.*

Olive is a ghost because she had unfinished business publishing a book. Now that we have a bestseller, I'm worried she might not be around much longer. I worry *I* might not be around much longer. And what about Seymour? How much longer do we have together as a family?

*I CAN'T ANSWER THAT. ALL I CAN SAY IS THAT NONE OF US WILL BE HERE FOREVER. WHAT'S WRONG, IGNATIUS? YOU'RE STANDING UP. ARE YOU GOING SOMEWHERE? ARE YOU LEAVING SPENCE MANSION?*

No. I'm staying right here. But I need to make sure I don't leave any unfinished business.

# IGNATIUS B. GRUMPLY

A WRITER IN RESIDENCE

September 15

Olive C. Spence
The Cupola
43 Old Cemetery Road
Ghastly, Illinois

Dear Olive,

I'm sorry I've been such a grump for so long. You'll be glad to know I've made a resolution to start smiling and laughing mor

Iggy, there's no need to keep apologizing. All is forgiven.

Thank you. But I have some news. I want to try something new.

Aha! So you're finally ready to stop being a neophobe and start being a neophiliac. Is that what you're trying to say?

What I want to say is very simple. Will you marry me, Olive?

*WHAT?*

You said you wanted me to come out of my shell and try new things. I'd get down on one knee and propose to you, but I can't very well type and kneel at the same time. I'll ask again. Olive, will you be my wife?

Is this a joke? Are you trying to be a punster, like your uncle Ian?

I've never been more serious in my life.

But we've never discussed marriage. You've never even mentioned it.

I know. I got the idea from Garren Teed.

Iggy, I think you have jet lag. You're tired from the long flight and talking crazy nonsense abou

This is where I interrupt you, Olive. Yes, I'm tired. I'm also old.

Not as old as me. Keep in mind I was born in 1818.

May I write without being interrupted?

I'm sorry. Please continue.

Thank you. What I'm trying to say is that relationships are *tough*. Getting along with another person is not always easy. In fact, it's hard. It can seem downright *impossible* at times, especially when you're a ghost who thinks I'm a ridiculous old tortoise. I'm not sure if I believe in monsters or sea serpents, but I believe in *you*, Olive. I believe in love. I don't know how much longer we have together, but however long it is, let's do this right. Let's get married. Is it too ridiculous? You can say something now. Anything. Please. Write something before I die of embarrassment.

No.

*No,* you won't marry me?

No, I don't think you're a ridiculous old tortoise. Do you think I'm crazy?

No. But I think you're dodging my question. Will you or won't you marry me?

Would it be legal? Is it even possible?

Anything's possible, Olive.

Of course. I *will* marry you, Iggy. But I'll still be a free spirit. And I insist on keeping my own last name.

Fine with me on both counts.

Let's have the wedding at Grumply Castle next summer. I'll wear a Victorian gown. You and Seymour can wear kilts.

Whoa, whoa, whoa.

Fortune favors the bold, Iggy.

We have almost a year to discuss this, right?

Yes. In the meantime, do you think we should tell Seymour?

I do.

I do, too. Won't this be fun? Oh, what's that? Someone's at the door. It's that man from the telegram company.

Not this again. Let's ignore it.

Iggy, answer the door! It must be important.

# INTERNATIONAL
# TELEGRAM SERVICE

**To:** RESIDENTS OF 43 OLD CEMETERY ROAD
**Fr:** THE QUEEN

## AN IMPORTANT MESSAGE
## FROM BUCKINGHAM PALACE

SEPTEMBER 15

HER ROYAL MAJESTY THE QUEEN OF
ENGLAND RESPECTFULLY REQUESTS
THAT YOU CHANGE THE NAME OF YOUR
LAUGHITORIUM = STOP = NEW NAME
SHOULD REFLECT THE FACT THAT THE
TORTOISE FORMERLY KNOWN AS MR
POE HAS ATTRACTED MORE THAN ONE
MILLION VISITORS TO LOCH NESS =
HENCE THE  LAUGHITORIUM IS NOT
THE HOME OF MR POE = STOP = IT
IS THE HOME OF SIR POE = STOP

4:58
PM

And so we leave Spence Mansion with the sound of laughter wafting through the windows.

As summer faded into fall, Ghastly's favorite family began making plans for an important day.

In keeping with tradition,
they would need something old.

And something Blew.

As children, author **Kate Klise** (left) and
illustrator **M. Sarah Klise** (right) were
lucky enough to visit Scotland on a family
vacation. They loved seeing the lush green
countryside and marveled at the mysterious
lakes, or "lochs."

They did not, however, see the Loch Ness
Monster. (Not on that trip, anyway).

Kate now looks for mysterious monsters
at her home in Norwood, Missouri. Sarah
searches for sea serpents and other creatures
at her home in Berkeley, California.

**www.kateandsarahklise.com**

# Is Laughing Really

* Yes! Laughing boosts the immune system and makes the body more resistant to disease.

* Laughing protects the heart.

* Laughing can relax the whole body.

* Laughing triggers the release of endorphins, which are the body's natural feel-good chemicals.